THE ANGEL with the GOLDEN GLOW

A family's journey through loss & healing

Written by **Elissa Al-Chokhachy**

Illustrated by **Ulrike Graf**

Once in a village in a faraway place, a child was born.

He was a child unlike any other child. He was special. Of course all babies are special, but this child was different. He was really an angel in disguise. His golden hair, long curly dark eyelashes, cherubic cheeks, and sweetness were the only telltale signs that could possibly give away his disguise.

This angel was full of courage, as are most angels who come to earth. Shortly before the cherub's birth, God gathered all the angels and held an important meeting in heaven.

"My beloved angels," He said, "how I love each of you for the joy you bring! Soon there is to be born on earth a special child. He will be different from other children in the things he will be able to do.

I need the bravest of all My cherubs to bring healing. You will be born in this special earthly body. It will not work in the same way as most do. Although you'll have loving parents, life will not be easy. Soon after your birth, they will know your time on earth will be brief."

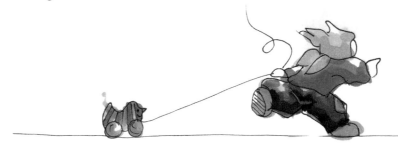

The cherubs started jumping up and down, waving their hands, hoping to be chosen! An angel's purpose is to spread love, joy, hope and healing. Each knows it is a great privilege to do God's work.

God looked among His angels and noticed one whose halo shone brighter than all the rest. "Little Angel with the Golden Glow," He announced, "I choose *you* to be born unto this earthly home. Your light is so bright it can penetrate even the deepest sadness and change it into love. It is you, blessed angel, who shall do My work on earth."

The angel was thrilled! How he had hoped he would be chosen! He would work with all his might to bring healing into his new home.

All the angels gathered around their friend to say goodbye. They would miss him. Yet they knew it was a great honor to be chosen for this wonderful journey.

One cherub, The Angel with the Tender Heart, was especially sad. He cried because The Angel with the Golden Glow was his best friend. What would he do without him? Sensing his friend's despair, The Angel with the Golden Glow hugged him close. As he did this, his halo shone so much light that his friend's sadness soon lifted.

"Don't be sad. This is the greatest day of my life. I'm off to share my love with the world. Remember I'll *always* love you... whether we are together or apart... one from the other. One day you too will be chosen, and then you'll understand."

When The Angel with the Golden Glow was finally ready, he was born into the chosen home. There was great celebration for he was the family's first child and first grandchild. His mom and dad and the entire family were ecstatic. And the child was loved immeasurably.

Shortly after his birth, the angel saw tears in the eyes of all who loved him. They had been told he was different. He would never be like other children. He would not stay on earth for very long. His family was sad. They hurt inside. They did not understand.

The Angel with the Golden Glow was puzzled. He knew he had been chosen for this very reason. If only he could explain. If only he could help in some way! Then he remembered his gift of the golden glow. From then on, whenever there was sadness, he shone his halo so brightly that the sadness disappeared. It magically turned into love... and his home overflowed with love!

The angel's parents loved him with all their hearts. His mom sang to him and gently caressed his body. She kissed him and said over and over, "I love you, my little snuggle-bunny. You're such a beautiful boy!" It was hard for his dad to leave to go to work. He wanted to spend every moment they had together. His dad would lie with his arm around him, and tell him, "I love you, son."

When their child was not able to do the things that other children could do, they loved him all the more. They were grateful he was in their lives, and thankful for all the joy he brought.

Sometimes his mom and dad, grandparents, aunts, uncles and cousins became sad again. They couldn't imagine what life would be like when he wasn't with them anymore. During those times, the angel beamed his halo the brightest until they felt better. The Angel with the Golden Glow felt happy inside. He felt fulfilled, for he knew he was doing all he had come to do.

Finally the day came when the angel's work on earth was completed. He was sad. He would miss his family, especially his mom and dad. He knew they would miss him too. Then he remembered that love never dies. They would always love one another. He also remembered there would be a time when they would be together again. This made him feel better. *How he loved them so...*

The Angel with the Golden Glow was gently and lovingly returned to heaven.

Once they were reunited, God said, "In you, child, I am well pleased." All the angels joyfully welcomed him and gave him a great celebration!

The Angel with the Golden Glow was elated to see his best friend. He told him all about his adventures on earth. "I had the most wonderful parents in all the world!" he exclaimed. The Angel with the Tender Heart listened to each and every story. How good it felt to be together again!

As The Angel with the Golden Glow finished telling his last story, his friend said, "I missed you so much. Yet our time together in heaven will be short. I have the most amazing news! God has chosen *me* to be born into the same family. There is still much healing that needs to be done. Just think! We will be earthly brothers as well as heavenly brothers. This is surely the greatest honor of my life!"

The Angel with the Golden Glow was happy for his friend's wonderful opportunity. There wasn't anyone in all of heaven he would rather send to his earth family than his dearest friend. Yet he would miss him. He had looked forward to the days when they would be together again.

As they hugged, The Angel with the Tender Heart felt his friend's sadness. His heart overflowed with so much love that the sadness disappeared! The two cherubs giggled in delight at the love that they shared and the special gifts they had been given. They felt happy and proud to be angels. Even though they would miss one another, it was okay. They understood. They knew how important it was for The Angel with the Tender Heart to go to earth.

As The Angel with the Tender Heart was leaving, he said, "I love you, dear friend. I promise to take tender loving care of all those you love on earth. Don't be sad... for there will be a day when we will be together again. And remember, as you so wisely taught me, I'll always love you... whether we are together or apart... one from the other."

In loving memory of Vail

"One who never said a word
but moved so many"

Published in the
United States of America by
Penny Bear Publishing
Six Elmwood Road
Marblehead, MA 01945
Printed in Singapore.
Book design by
Vail Edward Walter.

PEEF the Christmas Bear by Tom Hegg;
illustrated by Warren Hanson.
© 1995 Tom Hegg and Warren Hanson.
PEEF toy bear character illustrations
reproduced by permission of
Waldman House Press, Inc., Minneapolis,
Minnesota. All rights reserved.

Library of Congress
Cataloging-in-Publication Data
Al-Chokhachy, Elissa.
The angel with the golden glow:
A family's journey through loss & healing
by Elissa Al-Chokhachy;
illustrated by Ulrike Graf.
1st ed, p. cm.

SUMMARY: An angel is chosen
to be born as a special child,
who will be unable to do what
other children do, but who will
give his family healing in the
brief time he is with them.
LCCN: 98-96788
ISBN: 1-893356-00-0

1. Angels—Juvenile fiction.
2. Infants—Death—Religious aspects
—Juvenile fiction.
3. Grief— Religious aspects—Juvenile fiction.
I. Graf, Ulrike Andrea, 1973-, ill. II. Title.
PZ7.A3135An 1999 (E) QBI98-1658